TIMELESS CLASSICS

20,000 LEAGUES UNDER THE SEA

Jules Verne

– ADAPTED BY –

Emily Hutchinson

TIMELESS CLASSICS

Literature Set 1 (1719-1844)

A Christmas Carol
The Count of Monte Cristo
Frankenstein
Gulliver's Travels
The Hunchback of Notre Dame
The Last of the Mohicans

Oliver Twist
Pride and Prejudice
Robinson Crusoe
The Swiss Family Robinson
The Three Musketeers

Literature Set 2 (1845-1884)

The Adventures of Huckleberry Finn
The Adventures of Tom Sawyer
Around the World in 80 Days
Great Expectations
Jane Eyre
The Man in the Iron Mask

Moby Dick
The Prince and the Pauper
The Scarlet Letter
A Tale of Two Cities
20,000 Leagues Under the Sea

Literature Set 3 (1886-1908)

The Call of the Wild
Captains Courageous
Dracula
Dr. Jekyll and Mr. Hyde
The Hound of the Baskervilles
The Jungle Book

Kidnapped
The Red Badge of Courage
The Time Machine
Treasure Island
The War of the Worlds
White Fang

SADDLEBACK
EDUCATIONAL PUBLISHING
www.sdlback.com

ISBN-13: 978-1-61651-099-2
ISBN-10: 1-61651-099-4
eBook: 978-1-60291-833-7

Printed in the United States of America
15 14 13 12 11   1 2 3 4 5

Contents

| 1 |

A Bold Expedition

In the year 1866, a very strange thing happened. Several ships reported seeing an enormous "thing" in the ocean. Sometimes, the massive object seemed to be glowing. It was much larger and faster than a whale.

The captain of one ship thought it might be a sandbank. He was trying to figure out exactly where it was located. Then suddenly, the object started to shoot jets of water 150 feet into the air!

Three days later, the "thing" was spotted again. This time, it was several hundred miles away. Some people began to think it was a sea monster. They sang about it in cafes and made fun of it in newspapers.

Months later, the thing was no longer a scientific puzzle. It was a danger. A ship called the *Scotia* had been struck by it. Fortunately, the *Scotia* was divided into compartments. Only one compartment filled with water. When the damage was examined, a hole about two feet wide was found. Something had poked through the ship's thick iron plates! Whatever it was, the thing had to be incredibly strong.

I, Pierre Aronnax, am a professor at the Museum of Natural History in Paris. At this time, I was in America, as part of an expedition. Several people asked me what I thought about this strange thing at sea. Of course, I had already read a lot about the mysterious object. It was puzzling, but after much thought, I wrote an article about it.

I believed the thing might be an enormous sea animal. After all, many creatures of the deep are still unknown to us. I thought it might be a narwhal—a whale with a long, sharp tusk. The common narwhal is about 60 feet long. Its ivory tusk is as hard as steel. If the mysterious thing was a giant narwhal, it could probably pierce the hull of a ship.

My article was widely discussed. Many people believed that I'd solved the mystery.

Then I learned that an American ship had been asked to help. The *Abraham Lincoln* was going to chase down the creature and destroy it. I was asked to join the hunt.

What to do? I longed to return to Paris. I wanted to see my friends, my home, and my precious collections. But once I received the invitation, I forgot all that. I felt it was my destiny to rid the world of this monster. So, I quickly made up my mind to take the journey on the *Abraham Lincoln*.

Then I called out to Conseil, my devoted servant. In French, his name means "advice." But, in fact, Conseil never gave advice. For 10 years, he'd followed me wherever science led. And he'd never once complained about our long journeys. He'd always been ready to pack his bags for any country, from China to the Congo. And even better—he has good health, and no nerves. In 1866, this young man was 30 years old—and I was 40.

Conseil had only one fault. He would only speak to me in the third person. That odd habit was sometimes provoking.

"Did my master call?" Conseil asked.

"Yes, my boy," I said. "Make preparations for me and yourself, too. We will leave on another expedition in two hours."

"As you please, sir," Conseil said softly.

"We don't have an instant to lose," I said. "Put all my coats, shirts, and stockings in my trunk right away. Pack as much as you can for yourself, and be quick."

Conseil looked concerned. "We are not returning to Paris, then?" he asked.

"Oh! We will be returning to Paris," I said, "—but not right away."

"As my master wishes," Conseil said coolly.

"We're going after the famous narwhal," I explained. "Ridding it from the seas is a dangerous mission. But the ship's captain—Commander Farragut—is a daring man."

Our luggage was taken to the ship immediately. I hurried on board and asked for Commander Farragut. One of the sailors led me to a good-looking officer, who reached out to shake hands.

"Monsieur Pierre Aronnax?" he asked.

"Yes," I replied. "Commander Farragut?"

He nodded and said, "Welcome, Professor.

Your cabin has been made ready for you."

The *Abraham Lincoln*, a fast and powerful ship, had been well chosen for her mission. And Captain Farragut was worthy of her. To him, the unknown object of the sea was no mystery. He was certain it was a monster—and he had sworn to destroy it. Captain Farragut would either kill the narwhal, or the narwhal would kill the captain. In his mind, there was no third course.

All the officers on board shared their captain's opinion. They wanted nothing more than to meet the narwhal and kill it. Each one of them watched the seas eagerly.

Captain Farragut had offered his crew a reward. He'd promised $2,000 to the first sailor who spotted the monster.

I leave you to judge how well their eyes were used on board the *Abraham Lincoln*.

Captain Farragut had armed his ship well. He'd gathered every sort of gun and harpoon. Better still, Ned Land was on board. He was known as the prince of harpooners.

Ned Land was a Canadian, about 40 years old. He was a tall man, strongly built, serious, quiet—and occasionally violent. The look on his cunning face was bold. As a harpooner, he had no equal.

I didn't know him then, but we are old friends now. Our friendship was born from facing great danger together. Ah, brave Ned! I wish I had a hundred more years to live, so I could remember you longer!

Now, what were Ned Land's thoughts about the sea monster? I must admit that he didn't believe in the narwhal. He was the only one on board who held that opinion. Usually, he avoided the subject. But one evening, I pressed him to talk about it.

"Well, Ned," I said, "is it possible that you do not believe in the existence of the whale we are chasing? How can you be so incredulous?"

The harpooner looked at me for some moments before answering. "I've followed many a whale, sir. But none of them was strong enough to put even a scratch on the iron plate of a ship."

"Think about this, Ned," I said. "If such an animal exists, it would be extraordinarily strong. If it lived miles beneath the surface, it would likely have no equal in strength."

"Why is that?" Ned asked.

"We humans are used to the pressure of the air," I said. "But the pressure of the water is far, far greater. If we were taken any great distance beneath the waves, why, we would be crushed!"

"You've convinced me of one thing," Ned said. "If such animals do exist, they very well might be as strong as you say."

"All right," I went on. "And if they do *not* exist, how would you explain what happened to the *Scotia*?"

| 2 |

The Iron Monster

For a long time, the voyage of the *Abraham Lincoln* was uneventful. But one day in June, we were able to see a demonstration of Ned Land's amazing skill.

We'd met with an American whaling ship that day. Its crew knew we had Ned Land on board. They asked for his help with the whale they were chasing. Fate served the harpooner very well that day. Instead of one whale, he had harpooned two. And he'd struck one of them straight to the heart.

If a monster ever had to deal with Ned's harpoon, I wouldn't bet on the monster!

The crew was constantly on the lookout. They ate little and slept little. Twenty times a day, a sailor would call out that he saw the monster. But it was always a false alarm. The men were in a constant state of excitement.

For three months, the *Abraham Lincoln* traced back and forth across the waters of the North Pacific. In fact, the entire coast of the American continent was explored.

Finally, the crew decided the search was useless. Exhausted, they wanted nothing more than to return home. Captain Farragut asked them to hold on for three more days. If the monster wasn't found by then, the *Abraham Lincoln* would head for home.

Two days passed. A thousand schemes were tried to attract the monster's attention. A large amount of bacon was thrown overboard. The sharks feasted on it very well. The crew took off in small boats, searching everywhere. But nothing was found.

I urged Conseil to join the search. "Come, Conseil," I said. "This is your last chance to win 2,000 dollars."

"If I may say so," Conseil replied, "I don't think anyone will win that prize."

"You're probably right," I agreed. "This was a waste of time after all. We should've been back in France six months ago."

Conseil nodded. "If I had been working

in your museum, sir, I would already have classified all your fossils."

"As you say, Conseil. I suppose we shall be laughed at for our troubles," I sighed.

Then I heard Ned Land shouting, *"Look out there! I see it! I see it!"*

The entire crew—captain, officers, sailors, cabin boys—rushed toward Ned Land.

Under the water, we could see a great oval shape. The thing was glowing. I could tell the light was caused by electricity.

"It's moving!" I cried. "It's coming toward us!"

A great cry rose up from the crew.

"Silence!" the captain thundered. "Reverse the engines."

As the ship retreated, the thing came right behind her—moving twice as fast.

We gasped for breath. We stood frozen, unable to move as we watched the thing gaining on us. It made a circle around the ship, forming a ring like shining dust.

Then it sped off. Soon it was two or three miles away.

Commander Farragut turned to Ned Land. "If we came close enough, Mr. Land, would you try to harpoon it?" he asked.

"Certainly, sir," Ned replied.

"Make up your fires and put on all steam!" the captain called out to the engineer.

The crew cheered, knowing the time for attack had arrived. Clouds of black smoke poured out of the ship's smokestack.

The *Abraham Lincoln* went straight for the animal. The creature allowed the ship to come close—very close. Then it turned away.

We chased it for almost an hour, but we never got close enough to harpoon it.

"Engineer, put on more pressure," the captain said. Now, huge puffs of steam poured from the ship's valves. The ship was speeding forward at $18\frac{1}{2}$ miles an hour.

But the cursed animal swam just ahead of the *Abraham Lincoln*—at the very same speed.

For another hour, the ship kept up its chase. But it didn't gain an inch. A stubborn anger seized the crew. The captain twisted his beard, and then he began to chew it.

"We shall catch it!" Ned Land cried out. But just as he was about to let loose his harpoon, the animal sped farther away. A cry of furious frustration broke from the crew.

Hours passed. By then, the ship must have covered 300 miles. When night came on the animal finally stopped moving. *Perhaps it's tired at last*, I thought.

The captain gave his orders, and the *Abraham Lincoln* moved slowly toward the animal. Our eyes were dazzled by its electric glow. No one breathed. A deep silence fell on deck.

Ned Land raised his harpoon—and threw it! I heard the weapon strike something hard. The electric light went out. Suddenly two huge spouts of water arose from the sea and came crashing down on the deck. Water rushed from the front of the ship to the back, knocking men off their feet. Then everyone felt a great shock. Before I could stop myself, I was thrown over the rail and into the sea!

The darkness was intense. When I could see, the lights of the *Abraham Lincoln* were far in the distance. I was lost.

"Help! Help!" I cried out as I tried to swim toward the disappearing ship.

My clothes weighed me down. They seemed glued to my body. I was sinking! My mouth filled with water. I struggled, but the tide was pulling me under.

Suddenly, I felt myself being lifted above the waves. Someone was speaking these words in my ear: *If master would lean on my shoulder, master could swim more easily.*

"Conseil, is it you?" I gasped.

"It is," Conseil said. "I am waiting for my master's orders."

"Were you also thrown into the sea by the shock?" I sputtered.

"I wasn't," Conseil answered. "But as I am in my master's service, I jumped in after him."

I was not surprised that the worthy Conseil thought this was the natural thing to do.

"What happened to the *Abraham Lincoln*?" I asked when I caught my breath.

"I think that master had better not count on her," Conseil said. "I heard some men say her rudder was broken. That was the only damage. But the ship cannot turn around."

"Then there is no hope for us!" I wailed.

"Perhaps," Conseil said. "But we are not out of time yet—and one can accomplish a great deal in just a few hours."

Conseil's cool manner lifted my spirits. Perhaps the *Abraham Lincoln* would send a boat to look for us. We decided to swim toward it. This is how we managed: One of us would lie on his back, floating, while the other pushed him forward. Every 10 minutes or so, we would trade places. Although our chances were slim, I dared not lose hope.

Around one o'clock in the morning, I became terribly tired. My body stiffened with violent cramps. Conseil struggled to keep me afloat. I could hear him panting.

"Leave me!" I told him.

"Leave my master?" he cried. "*Never!* I would drown first."

Just then the moon appeared. In its beams, I saw the ship. It was about five miles away.

I tried to cry out. But no sound escaped from my swollen lips.

"Help! Help!" Conseil began yelling.

An indistinct sound seemed to answer him.

"Did you hear that?" I murmured.

"Yes! Yes!" Conseil said.

This time there was no mistake. Again, a faint human voice was calling out to us!

Conseil began towing me toward the voice. My strength was gone. Extreme cold crept into my bones, and I began to sink.

Then my feet struck a hard surface. By the light of the moon, I saw a face I recognized.

"Ned! Thank God, it's you!" I cried. "Were you also thrown into the sea?"

"Yes, sir, I was," Ned answered. "But I was luckier than you. I found a place to stand. We're on top of the monster right now. And now I know why my harpoon didn't enter its skin."

"Why, Ned, why?" I asked.

"Because, Professor, the monster is made of iron," Ned said.

I stomped my feet. The blow made a metallic sound. Then I understood. We were on the back of some sort of submarine.

The thing rose out of the water. I heard a noise come from inside. Then an iron plate was moved aside, and a man appeared. He let out an odd cry and quickly vanished.

Some moments later, eight men wearing masks came out and took us inside.

| 3 |

Aboard the *Nautilus*

We must have slept for 24 hours. When we finally woke, we were terribly hungry. Ned Land was especially eager to be fed.

"Patience, Master Land," Conseil said. "We must follow the rules of this vessel. It may not be dinnertime yet."

"That is just like you, friend Conseil," Ned laughed. "You are never out of temper. I believe you would die of hunger rather than make a complaint!"

We waited for hours in the room where we had slept. When no one appeared, I became nervous. Conseil, however, stayed calm. Had we been saved, or had we been kidnapped? Who could tell?

Finally, a servant came in. Roaring in fury, Ned Land sprang up and seized the fellow by the throat.

Conseil and I rushed to the servant's rescue. Then a voice behind us said in French: "Be quiet, Master Land. And you, Professor—will you please listen to me?"

A stranger stood before us. At a sign from him, the servant staggered out of the room.

"I would have spoken to you sooner," the stranger went on, "but I wanted to know who you were. Now I see that you are Mr. Pierre Aronnax, professor of the Natural History Museum of Paris. This man is your servant, Conseil. And that man is Ned Land, the well-known harpooner.

"I've been wondering what to do with you," the stranger continued. "Your ship has attacked me, after all. That means, as the commander of this vessel, I have the right to treat you as enemies."

"But, sir," I objected, "your submarine has been a subject of great concern. Why, all of Europe and America have considered you a danger! In fact, we actually believed that your submarine was a sea monster!"

"Ha!" the stranger scoffed. "If you'd known the monster was actually a submarine,

I'm sure you would still have attacked me!"

I had no answer to this. The stranger was entirely correct.

"Then you understand, sir," the stranger went on, "that I'm entitled to regard you as enemies. If I wished, I could place you on the deck and sink the submarine. That would be my right, wouldn't it?"

"It might be the right of a *savage*," I cried, "but not the right of a civilized man!"

"Ah, but I am *not* a civilized man!" the stranger said. "I've cut myself off from society, and I do not obey its laws!"

Hot anger flashed in the stranger's eyes. There was a long silence before he continued. "After some thought, I've made a decision. I will allow you to stay on board after all. But there's one condition: You may have to remain in your cabins at certain times. There may be events that you will not be allowed to see. But apart from this condition, you will be free to come and go—but only on board the submarine."

"Pardon me, sir," I said, "but that is the freedom a prisoner has to walk about his prison. That cannot be enough for us."

"It *must* be enough," he said firmly.

"What!" I cried. "We must never see our country or our friends or our families again? You can't mean it! That is cruelty!"

"No, sir," he said. "I am sparing your lives. When you attacked me, you uncovered a secret that was never to be known—the fact that I exist. Now that you know my secret, do you think I would set you free? Never!

"I've read some of your books on the sea, Professor. You know a great deal—but you don't know *everything*. I'm quite sure you won't regret your time here. You're going to learn about the land of marvels."

With that argument, he'd touched my weak point. All right, then. I would trust the future to decide the question of my freedom.

"What is your name, sir?" I asked.

"I am nothing to you but Captain Nemo," he replied. "And you and your friends are passengers on the *Nautilus*."

Then Captain Nemo had a servant lead Ned Land and Conseil to their cabins. Breakfast would be served to them there. I would have breakfast with the captain.

He led me to a handsome dining room. Lovely paintings hung on the walls. The table gleamed with silver utensils.

The food was quite good, but I could not tell what I was eating.

"My cook is a very clever fellow," Captain Nemo said. "What you believe is meat, is actually turtle. And these dolphin livers taste exactly like pork. Everything we eat is harvested from the sea."

"You like the sea, Captain?" I asked.

"I *love* the sea!" he roared. "The sea is everything. It covers seven-tenths of the globe. It is a great desert, where man is never lonely. The sea is peace. It has no rulers. On earth, men make unjust laws. They fight and tear each other to pieces. But thirty feet below the waves, men have no power. I have no masters in the sea. I am free!"

As he spoke, Captain Nemo had become very excited. Now, he calmed himself and politely invited me to tour the *Nautilus*.

First, we visited the library, which was filled with books in every language.

Another room was like an art museum. Captain Nemo had collected the fine pictures for years. "These are my last souvenirs of a world that is dead to me," he said.

The captain's collections of shells and pearls were in another part of the room. I saw pink pearls, green pearls, yellow, blue, and black pearls. Some of these were larger than a pigeon's egg—no doubt worth millions!

Captain Nemo showed me my room, which was elegant. His own room was quite plain. On his wall were several instruments. He explained that some were used to determine the *Nautilus*'s position at sea. Others gauged the temperature and the weather. There was also a manometer, which showed the depth and pressure of the water.

Then he told me something that surprised me very much: the *Nautilus* was powered by electricity. Captain Nemo had devised a way to use the chemicals in sea water and other natural resources to produce electrical energy.

"Electricity gives us heat and light," he said. "And it also propels the *Nautilus* forward. As I told you before, everything comes from the ocean."

"But not the air you breathe?" I asked.

"For air, I go up to the water's surface," he said. "I store a good supply of air in huge reservoirs. After they're full, I can stay underwater as long as I like."

We walked around the *Nautilus* for some time. At the center was a boat, which was sometimes used for fishing. There was an engine room stocked with the materials used to make electricity. A powerful propeller was also there. At the front of the submarine was a long spur—as sharp as a sword. I realized that it was this spur that must have pierced the hull of the *Scotia*.

The *Nautilus* was exactly 232 feet long. It had two hulls made of steel plates—strong enough to withstand the great pressure of deep water. To sink the submarine to the bottom, special chambers were filled with water.

"Your *Nautilus* is certainly a marvelous boat," I said. "How did you build it in secret?"

"I had my workshops set up on a desert island," Captain Nemo replied. "It was there I taught the workmen how to put it together. When the work was finished, we burned every trace of our construction project."

"The *Nautilus* must have cost a great deal. Are you rich, Captain Nemo?" I asked.

"Immensely rich, sir," the captain said. "I could pay the national debt of France and never miss the money."

I stared at him in awe. Could this man possibly be serious? Only the future could answer that question.

| 4 |

Underwater Adventures

We began our journey in the Pacific Ocean. Now the *Nautilus* was following one of the great ocean currents—called the Black River—along the coast of Asia.

I could tell that Ned Land was thinking of escaping. "Can you tell me how many men are on board, Mr. Aronnax?" he asked.

"I don't know, Mr. Land," I said. "But this is not a good time to plot an escape. The *Nautilus* is a masterpiece of modern science! I would be sorry not to have seen it. So, let's accept our situation—and enjoy it! Be quiet now and let's see what happens."

"*See?*" Ned Land cried out in exasperation. "We can see nothing in this iron cage. We are traveling blindly."

Ned Land had hardly finished speaking when the room suddenly went dark. Stunned and silent, we heard a smooth, sliding noise. It sounded like panels on a track.

"This is the end of us!" Ned Land wailed.

Then lights on each side of the room came on. Two big panels had been pulled back from the wall! Now we were looking out huge windows at the deep sea itself. It was as if we were in front of an immense aquarium!

Ned Land forgot his ill temper at the wonder of the sight.

A parade of fish passed by—beautiful, bright, and swift. There were mackerel with blue bodies and silver heads; goby fish with violet spots; serpents six feet long, with small, lively eyes. Every fish of the China Sea swam before our dazzled eyes.

For two hours, Ned named the fish, and Conseil classified them. Then, without warning, the panels slowly closed. I sat there for a long time, thinking about all I had seen.

That evening I spent reading, writing, and thinking until sleep overpowered me.

The next day was the ninth of November. I wanted to talk to Captain Nemo, but for some reason, we didn't see him for several days.

Then I found a note from the captain in my room. He invited my friends and me to a hunting party. He said it would take place in the forests on the Island of Crespo.

"A hunt!" Ned exclaimed happily. "The captain is actually going to set foot on land?"

"That's what it sounds like," I said. I was surprised, for I had also understood that Captain Nemo hated the very thought of land.

"Well, then, we must accept," Ned said. "I shall be glad to eat some fresh venison."

We were astonished to find that the Island of Crespo was deep in the sea.

Captain Nemo explained that we'd wear special diving suits. On our backs, we'd carry air-filled packs outfitted with breathing tubes. Our guns were air guns, and the bullets were made of glass.

When Ned Land saw the diving suits, he refused to put one on. "Unless I'm forced, I will never wear that!" he sputtered.

"No one will force you, Master Ned," the captain assured him.

"Is Conseil going to risk it?" Ned asked.

Conseil raised his eyebrows. "I follow my

master wherever he goes," he replied.

The diving suits were heavy and tough enough to resist the pressure of the deep ocean. The pants ended in heavy boots. On our heads we wore metal helmets that had viewing panels made of thick glass. With my backpack of air, I could breathe easily.

I had an electric lamp in one hand and a gun in the other. But I couldn't move a step in my heavy suit! Then I felt myself being pushed into a little room. When a watertight door closed, we were wrapped in darkness.

After some minutes, we heard a loud hissing. I felt cold water rising from my feet to my chest. When the room was filled with water, another door opened and we stepped out onto the ocean floor.

After a few steps, I no longer felt the weight of my suit. What wonders I saw! There were rocks, shells, plants, and sea animals of every color. It was a perfect kaleidoscope of green, yellow, orange, violet, and blue!

The ocean floor was blanketed with coral, fungus, anemones, and starfish. I hated to crush so many lovely specimens under my feet. But we had to walk, so we went ahead.

Captain Nemo was in the lead. After a while, he stopped and pointed.

This must be the forest, I thought.

Like trees, the dense sea plants around us reached up from the bottom to the surface of the ocean. There were no branches. Each plant grew as straight as an iron rod.

We rested in the forest for a while. I wished I could speak to the others. I looked at Conseil, and his eyes were shining with delight.

After four hours of walking, we came to a wall of rocks. We'd reached the edge of the Island of Crespo. Above us was the earth! Captain Nemo stopped abruptly. This was the end of his territory. He would go no farther.

As we headed back toward the *Nautilus*, Captain Nemo suddenly raised his gun, aimed, and fired. At some distance from us, a magnificent sea otter fell. Its pelt would have been very valuable, for it was five feet long, and its coat was beautiful.

An hour or so later, I was glad to see the lights of the *Nautilus*. I was walking a few steps behind Captain Nemo when he suddenly reached out and pushed me to the ground. Then he lay down beside me.

Just then, an enormous shadow passed over us. Two sharks! Knowing how easily they could crush us in their iron jaws, I shuddered. Luckily for us, however, sharks don't see well. In a moment they passed by, brushing us with their fins.

Half an hour later, we were back in the *Nautilus*. Being tired and hungry, I hurried to my room. My head was filled with wonder at our visit to the bottom of the sea.

| 5 |

Shipwrecks and Sharks

The next morning was the 18th of November. I was on the platform of the *Nautilus*, admiring the ocean, when Captain Nemo appeared. He didn't seem to notice me. Several crewmembers were also on the platform. They pulled in fishing nets that had been laid out the night before. These strong, healthy men seemed to come from many different nations. I recognized Irishmen, Frenchmen, and a Greek. Among themselves, they all spoke an odd language I didn't understand.

As the days passed, I saw very little of Captain Nemo. The *Nautilus* was heading southeast. On the 27th of November, we passed the island of Hawaii. In these waters, the sailors' nets brought up beautiful fish, some with azure fins and tails like gold.

On the 11th of December, I was reading a

book when Conseil interrupted me.

"Will master come here for a moment?" he asked. I noticed that his face was pale. "I want you to see something."

I followed him to the open panels. A huge, dark shape was lying on the ocean floor. "Why, it's a ship!" I cried.

The wreck must have happened only a few hours earlier. Five corpses were still lying on the deck—four men and a woman. And the woman held a baby in her arms!

Our hearts beat fast as we stared at the sad scene of life's last moments. Then huge sharks with hungry eyes came into view. They were heading toward the wreckage!

A moment later, the *Nautilus* circled the sunken ship. Now I could read its name: the *Florida*. I turned away from the horror.

This terrible sight was the first of many. We saw not only the hulls of more wrecked ships, but scattered debris including rusty cannons, bullets, and anchors.

On the 25th of December, Christmas day, we sailed near the New Hebrides. Ned Land was very sad that day. He said he missed the celebration of Christmas very much.

On January 1st, Conseil came to me. "Will master allow me to wish him a happy New Year?" he asked.

"What do you mean?" I grumbled. "Do you mean the year that will bring an end to our imprisonment? Or is this the year we continue on this strange voyage?"

As always, Conseil stayed positive. "I don't know how to answer," he said. "We are sure to see curious things. I don't know how our journey will end. Seeing everything would make it a happy year for me."

Captain Nemo's plan was to reach the Indian Ocean by crossing the Strait of Torres. This would be difficult, for the straits were full of small islands and giant rocks. The *Nautilus* went forward slowly. All around her, the sea dashed furiously.

Then the tide began to drop. The *Nautilus* was about two miles from an island when a great shock knocked me over. Oh, no! The submarine had struck something.

Captain Nemo, cool and calm as always, told me what had happened. The *Nautilus* was caught between coral rocks. She wasn't damaged, but she was stuck.

"Will this force you to live on land now?" I asked the captain.

Captain Nemo looked at me curiously. "Our voyage has only begun," he said. "I would hate to lose you as a passenger so soon. But in five days the full moon will raise the tide enough to set the *Nautilus* afloat."

Ned Land watched Captain Nemo leave. "Professor," he said, "this piece of iron will *never* leave these rocks! I think the time has come for us to leave Captain Nemo."

"Friend Ned," I said, "escape might be desirable if we were close enough to England or France. But we're on the shores of New Guinea! We know nothing of the natives here. How would they treat us?"

"But it's an island," he went on, "with trees and game. Think of it—we'll have meat!"

"Friend Ned is right," Conseil agreed. "Could master get permission to go on land— if only to feel the earth beneath our feet?"

"I can ask him," I said doubtfully. "But I'm quite sure he'll refuse."

To my great surprise, Captain Nemo agreed. And he didn't make us promise to return. I knew, though, that traveling in New Guinea might be dangerous. Perhaps it was better to be a prisoner on board than to risk falling into the hands of hostile natives.

Soon Ned and I set off in the small boat, armed with hatchets and guns. Ned was full of joy—like an escaped prisoner. *"Meat!"* he cried out. "We're finally going to eat some fresh meat!"

We left the boat on a sandy beach. Ned lovingly touched the soil with his feet. We hadn't set foot on land in two months.

The island was covered with tall forests. Some of the trees must have been 200 feet tall! Lush orchids and ferns grew everywhere.

But Ned Land didn't notice the beautiful specimens. Discovering a coconut tree, he beat down some of the fruit. We drank the milk and eagerly ate the tender pulp.

"Excellent!" Ned Land said happily. Then he suggested taking a load of coconuts back on board the *Nautilus*.

But Conseil had a better idea: "We should

save three places in our boat: one for fruit, one for vegetables, and a third for meat."

Next we found a breadfruit tree. Ned knew how to prepare this treat. He lit a fire while Conseil and I chose the best fruits. These had thick skin covering a white pulp. Ned sliced the breadfruit and roasted them. The flavor tasted much like an artichoke.

After eating the breadfruit, we gathered beans, yams, and several more coconuts. That evening, we returned to the *Nautilus*.

We saw no one on board the next morning, so we set off again for the island. Ned was determined to find some meat. We saw birds of paradise, but our shots missed when we fired at them. Finally, Conseil shot two pigeons, which we roasted and ate.

But Ned said he wouldn't be happy until he'd shot four-footed game. And *I* wouldn't be happy until I'd bagged a bird of paradise.

An hour later, Conseil did bring me a bird of paradise. Strangely, he'd found it lying on the ground, drunk from eating nutmegs!

Around two o'clock, Ned shot a magnificent hog. He skinned and cleaned it, and

we carried off the meat. Then we found a herd of small kangaroos, called "kangaroo rabbits." Ned killed a half dozen of them.

Dinner was excellent. We ate roast pig, mangos, coconuts, pineapples, and more.

"Suppose we stay here tonight, instead of returning to the *Nautilus*," Conseil suggested.

"Suppose we *never* return?" Ned said.

Just then a stone fell at our feet.

| 6 |

Captain Nemo's Secret

Conseil looked around. "Stones do not fall from the sky," he said.

Then a second stone fell, knocking a pigeon leg from Conseil's hand. We jumped up and held our guns at the ready.

"Are they apes?" Ned Land cried out.

"No, they're savages," Conseil replied.

"To the boat!" I shouted.

About 20 natives, armed with bows and arrows and rocks, then stepped out of the trees. Stones and arrows flew at us.

Ned Land carried pig meat in one arm and kangaroos in the other. In two minutes, we were on the beach. We loaded the boat and pushed off in an instant. The savages chased after us until the water reached their waists.

Some 20 minutes later, we were back at the *Nautilus*. Again, the platform was deserted.

I went inside and found Captain Nemo bent over the keys of his pipe organ. Lovely music filled the room.

"Captain!" I said.

He went on playing.

"Captain!" I shouted, touching his hand.

He shuddered and turned around.

"There are savages close by," I said.

"Savages?" he sneered. His tone was very sarcastic. "Why are you surprised at finding savages? There are savages on every land on earth. And why do you call *these* people savages? How do you know that they're any worse than most people?"

"But, Captain—" I began.

"Mr. Aronnax," said Captain Nemo, "the *Nautilus* has nothing to fear if they attack." With that, he returned to his music.

Nothing happened during the night. Perhaps the savages were frightened by the strange-looking submarine. After all, the panels of the *Nautilus* were open; they could easily have entered it.

At dawn the next morning, I went up to the platform. There was a huge crowd of savages now—perhaps 500. Some of them had walked far out onto the coral, so I could see them clearly. They had athletic bodies, shining and black. Their hair was woolly, with a reddish tinge. Bones hung from their ears. The men were naked and the women wore skirts made from big leaves. The chiefs had collars of glass beads, red and white. Almost all were armed with bows and arrows. Others carried slings for hurling stones.

A man of high rank, who wore banana leaves, came very close. I could have knocked him down, but I did not. I waited to see what he planned to do.

When the tide was low, they roamed around the *Nautilus*. Several times they gestured for me to go on land, but I did not.

Later that morning I decided to take the boat out to hunt for rare sea life. I called Conseil, and we went to work. For two hours, we searched, but found nothing rare. We did find some sea slugs, oysters, and small turtles for the *Nautilus*'s cook to prepare.

Then, just when I least expected it, my hand fell on a rare wonder. I cried out.

"What's the matter, sir?" Conseil asked. "Has master been bitten?"

"Oh, no," I said. "But I would have given a finger for this." I held up a precious shell.

"But it is a common shell," Conseil said.

"Not so," I said. "Look closely. Instead of being rolled from right to left, this one turns from left to right."

We had found a real treasure! Serious shell collectors would pay their weight in gold for such a prize! I promised myself to donate it to the museum when I returned to Paris.

We were gazing at the shell when a rock suddenly smashed it. I was aghast. One of the savages had destroyed it!

Conseil took up his gun. Before I could stop him, his shot shattered a bracelet on the savage's arm.

"Conseil!" I cried out.

"Well," he said, "it seems clear that the savages have begun the attack!"

"A shell isn't worth a man's life," I scolded.

"The scoundrel!" Conseil cried. "I'd rather he'd broken my shoulder than the shell!"

Conseil was serious—but I didn't agree.

Our situation had changed, however. By now, some 20 canoes surrounded the *Nautilus*.

As we neared the submarine, a shower of arrows rained down on us.

Once inside, I hurried to find Captain Nemo. "Sir," I said, "we must close the hatches."

"Nothing could be simpler," he replied. Then he pressed a button, which sent an order to the crew.

"But what about tomorrow?" I asked. "By then we must open the hatches to let in air. How will we keep the savages away?"

"Well, sir," Captain Nemo said, "let them come if they must. I wouldn't take a single life in order to stop them."

All night, the savages stamped on the platform, making loud cries. The crew seemed to take no notice of them.

When I arose the next morning, I saw that the hatches were still closed. We were now breathing air from the reservoirs.

At about half-past two, I went to see Captain Nemo. If he was correct, in 10 minutes the high tide would lift the *Nautilus* from the coral rocks.

As the hatches yawned opened, Ned Land, Conseil, and I saw a crowd of angry natives. One eager fellow touched the stair rail. Then, with a loud cry of rage, he pulled his hand away and ran off.

Ten more savages tried to come up the stairs. They too cried out before turning away and running off. Curious, Ned Land approached the staircase. He, too, was knocked off his feet when he seized the rail.

He shrieked like the others and then cried out, "I'm struck by a thunderbolt!"

This explained it all. The stair rail was actually a metal cable charged with electricity!

As the savages retreated to the island, we tried our best to comfort Ned Land.

A moment later—just as Nemo had predicted—the *Nautilus* rose up on the tide and drifted free! Her propeller moved slowly, then faster and faster. Soon the coral rocks were left behind.

The days passed. We lived like snails in our shells. It is very easy to lead a snail's life.

Then, on the 18th of January, a strange thing happened. I went on the platform and saw Captain Nemo and his second lieutenant talking. The lieutenant seemed disturbed. Both men were staring into the distance. I looked in the same direction, but could see nothing but water. Then Captain Nemo ordered the engineer to go faster.

I found a telescope and was about to peer through it when Captain Nemo snatched it from my hand. I turned to him, surprised. The look on his face had completely changed. His eyes flashed. His teeth were set. His head had shrunk down between his shoulders.

Was he angry at me? No—his eyes were fixed on that same faraway spot.

Finally, he spoke. "Mr. Aronnax," he said, "you must now abide by the condition I set when you came on board. You will stay in your cabin until I give orders to release you."

What could I do? "You are the master," I said. "But may I ask one question?"

"None, sir," he said, as he turned away.

After we were given breakfast, Ned Land and Conseil fell into a heavy sleep. I, too, had trouble keeping my eyes open. It seemed that Captain Nemo had drugged our food. Though

I tried to stay awake, I too feel deeply asleep.

When I awoke, I was in my own bunk. The *Nautilus* was as quiet as ever.

About two o'clock, Captain Nemo came to my cabin. He looked very tired. "Are you a doctor, Mr. Aronnax?" he asked.

When I replied that I was, he asked me to look at one of his sailors. Then he led me to a man about 40 years of age.

The man's head was wrapped in bandages. When I undid them, I saw that the poor fellow wouldn't live long. His skull had been shattered by some deadly weapon, and his brain was damaged.

"What caused this wound?" I asked.

Captain Nemo didn't answer.

"He'll be dead in two hours," I said quietly. "Nothing can save him."

To my surprise, I saw tears in the captain's eyes. He sent me away.

The next morning, Captain Nemo asked if I would like to take another walk beneath the sea. I quickly agreed.

This time, Ned Land joined us, as well as a dozen or so of Captain Nemo's men.

Soon we came to a marvelous place called the coral kingdom. Here, delicate sea creatures lived in colonies like animated flowers. The coral formations were fantastic.

Captain Nemo stopped. His men formed a semicircle around him. I then saw that four of them were carrying an oblong box.

A cross made of coral stood on a mound of rocks. When the captain made a sign, two of the men came forward. A few feet from the cross, they began to dig with an axe. I understood! The place was a cemetery, and the hole a tomb. Inside the box was the body of the man who had died.

"Now he is buried, forgotten by everyone but us," Captain Nemo said sadly. "Here he will be safe from sharks—and safe from men at last."

| 7 |

The Underwater Tunnel

We had now come to the second part of our journey. The first had ended with the moving scene in the coral cemetery.

My theory about Captain Nemo had changed. But Conseil believed that he was a misunderstood genius who'd turned away from society to save himself. In my eyes shunning society wasn't enough for him. I'd begun to suspect that he was really after revenge. In the past some terrible wrong must have been done to him.

As we entered the Indian Ocean, Captain Nemo came to my cabin. He invited me to join him in a hunt for pearls near Ceylon.

"Certainly, Captain," I said.

But then he frowned and studied my face. "You aren't afraid of sharks, are you?" he asked.

When I said I was not very familiar with

sharks, Captain Nemo assured me that we would be well armed. But the question had unnerved me.

Ned, however, was quite willing to face sharks. And Conseil vowed that he would be by my side whatever the danger.

Early the next morning, we put on diving suits and set out. We were armed only with daggers. Captain Nemo led us through an enormous oyster bed. But we didn't stop there. After moving down a steep slope, the captain pointed to an amazing object. It was a truly gigantic oyster—more than two and a half yards wide!

The oyster's shell was slightly ajar. Captain Nemo quickly slipped his dagger inside the shell to keep it from closing. Then he gently pulled back the oyster's flesh so I could see inside. Here was a perfect, shining pearl the size of a coconut! I put out my hand to touch it. But the captain caught my eye and shook his head. Then I understood. He was leaving the pearl in place so it would grow even larger.

We walked on for 10 minutes or so before Captain Nemo stopped again. About five yards away, we could see a shadow. It was a man, an Indian, diving for pearls. Just overhead, I could see the bottom of his canoe. I noticed that a stone was tied between the man's feet. Apparently, the weight of it helped him reach the bottom quickly. He was using a rope, which was attached to his boat, to lower himself and then haul himself back up.

For a few minutes, we watched him work. He would gather up about 10 oysters and then dive again. Then, suddenly, he recoiled in terror. A gigantic shark was rushing toward him! Luckily, the shark's tail only struck his chest as the Indian threw himself to one side.

The shark turned, ready to attack again. Captain Nemo reacted immediately. Dagger in hand, he quickly stepped in front of the fearsome beast. When the shark lunged, Captain Nemo, with wonderful quickness, turned aside. At the same moment he thrust his dagger into the shark's side.

The water turned red with blood. Then, hanging onto one of the shark's fins, Captain Nemo stabbed the shark again and again. But somehow the beast fought on.

Finally, Captain Nemo lost his grip and fell to the bottom. As the shark's jaws opened wide, Ned Land rushed forward with his harpoon. His mighty thrust struck the beast in the heart. As it died, the huge creature thrashed about dreadfully.

The captain went straight for the Indian. First, he cut the rope that bound the stone to his feet. Then he took the man in his arms and swam to the surface.

The rest of us, of course, followed him to the man's boat.

We all watched as the Indian slowly opened his eyes. He must have been terrified to see four copper helmets bent over him! And imagine his surprise when Captain Nemo placed a bag of pearls in his hand. The man's hands trembled as he accepted the gift. His eyes were filled with wonder.

Later, I couldn't stop thinking about what Captain Nemo had done. *He'd said that he was finished with the human race—yet he'd risked his life for a stranger.*

We entered the Red Sea on February ninth. Captain Nemo announced that in two days, we would reach the Mediterranean.

"The Mediterranean in two days!" I exclaimed. I was astonished.

Then Captain Nemo explained that he'd discovered an underwater tunnel. By traveling through it, the *Nautilus* would go beneath Suez and directly into the Mediterranean.

As we approached the tunnel, we saw an enormous creature floating on the sea. It was a dugong—a huge, flippered mammal related to the manatee.

Ned Land was eager to hunt it down, so Captain Nemo offered him a harpoon and his boat. Along with some of the captain's crew, we set off immediately.

At first, the dugong seemed to be sleeping. But as we came closer, it woke up and dove. We chased the dugong for an hour. Then it turned and headed toward the boat.

"Look out!" Ned shouted.

The dugong threw itself upon us. In seconds, it buried its teeth in the side of the boat and lifted it out of the water! Except for Ned Land, we all tumbled over one another. He, however, hung onto the front of the boat.

A moment later, his deadly harpoon was buried in the creature's heart.

It took a great deal of strength to hoist the dugong on board. The enormous animal must have weighed 10,000 pounds!

The next day, the *Nautilus* went under the waves. Captain Nemo himself guided it toward a large opening, black and deep. The *Nautilus* was entering the tunnel that Captain Nemo had described! The strange roaring in our ears was the sound of rushing water as we shot forward with the current, swift as an arrow.

In less than 20 minutes, we were in the Mediterranean!

| 8 |

Captain Nemo's Good Deed

On the 12th of February, the *Nautilus* rose to the surface. I hurried to the platform, along with Ned and Conseil.

"We're on the Mediterranean!" Ned Land cried out. "Good! Now, before Captain Nemo drags us any farther, let's plan our escape."

Although I didn't want to leave, I didn't wish to hold my friend back. My studies of the deep ocean were nearly done. But would I ever have another chance to see the wonders of the depths? Certainly not.

"Friend Ned," I said, "are you so tired of being on board?"

Ned looked thoughtful. "I don't regret this undersea journey," he answered. "But now that it is done, it's time to go."

"For me," I said, "it won't come to an end

until I have nothing more to learn from these seas. Perhaps we'll come close to the coasts of France, England, or America. I'd rather escape to one of those places."

Ned shook his head. "Mr. Aronnax," he said, "your arguments are rotten. You speak of the future. I speak of the present. After all, we live in the here and now. We must take advantage while we can."

"Perhaps you're right," I said. "We cannot depend on Captain Nemo's good will. It is prudent for him to keep us here. And it is prudent for us to take advantage of a chance to leave. But our first attempt *must* succeed. If it fails, we may not have another chance. The captain won't forgive us. But tell me, Ned—just *how* would you escape?"

"It should be a dark night, and we should be close to shore," Ned said.

So far, I didn't disagree. "And you plan to escape by swimming?" I asked.

"Yes," Ned said. "Or—if we're quite a long way from the coast—we could take the submarine's small boat."

"Let's not speak another word of this,"

I cautioned him. "The day you are ready, come and let us know. Then we will follow you."

To Ned Land's great disappointment, the next two days brought no chance of escape. Did Captain Nemo distrust us—even with so many ships around? I couldn't tell. But we were often deep beneath the surface, or many miles from shore.

On the 14th of February, we were headed toward the island of Crete. When we had sailed on the *Abraham Lincoln*, the island had been in an uproar. The people there had risen up against the harsh rule of the Turks.

Captain Nemo and I were watching the sea through the open panels. The captain seemed to be waiting for something. Suddenly a man appeared, swimming with a strong stroke.

"There's been a shipwreck!" I cried out. "We must save that fellow at any price!"

Captain Nemo didn't answer me. Instead, he signaled the swimmer, who promptly responded with a hand signal of his own. Then he rose to the surface and swam away.

"Don't worry," Captain Nemo said. "That man is Nicholas Pesca. He's a bold diver who regularly swims from one island to another. Sometimes he even goes as far as Crete."

Then the captain showed me a sort of strongbox. Inside were a great many ingots—of pure gold! Where did this gold come from? And what was he going to do with it?

I watched as Captain Nemo removed the ingots, one by one. He placed them in a chest bound with iron. When the chest was fastened, I watched him write an address on the box. The words were Greek.

Next he signaled two crewmembers to take the box away. When he finally said good night, I was left to wonder: *What was the connection between the diver and the chest filled with gold?*

On the 18th of February, we entered the Atlantic Ocean. Ned Land approached me. "We will escape tonight, at nine o'clock," he said. "By then, we should be only a few miles from the coast of Spain. It is cloudy. The sea is rough. But the small boat is strong. I have your word, Mr. Aronnax."

There was nothing I could say. He was right. This was an almost perfect chance.

The next hours were dreadful. Sometimes I envisioned myself and my friends safely on shore. Sometimes I wished that something would happen to prevent our escape.

At seven o'clock, dinner was served—but I could hardly eat. At eight o'clock, I dressed warmly. Somehow I felt as if an invisible eye was reading my secret thoughts. At a few minutes to nine, I stood at the door of the captain's room, listening. But I could hear nothing.

Then I felt a slight shock. We were at the bottom of the ocean. Something unusual was going on! I grew very anxious. There was no signal from Ned Land.

A moment later, Captain Nemo appeared. He led me toward the room with the open panels. Looking out, I saw men from the *Nautilus* in their diving suits. They were opening half-rotted cases left behind after a long ago shipwreck. And from these cases, they were removing ingots of gold and silver, as well as fabulous jewels!

Then I remembered that Spanish ships had sunk on this very spot in 1702. They'd been carrying money to the Spanish government.

I also realized that—for tonight at any rate—escape would be out of the question.

"This is but one of a thousand ships that have sunk," Captain Nemo said. "Now can you see where I got my great wealth?"

"I do not pity the wealthy people who lost such riches," I said. "But I do pity the poor, who might have been helped by this money."

Captain Nemo frowned in irritation. "Do you think I gather these riches for myself alone?" he snarled. "Do you suppose that I'm ignorant of the suffering people on this earth? Do you not understand?"

Suddenly, I *did* understand. I realized that the gold Captain Nemo had loaded in the iron-bound chest would be given to the poor people of war-torn Crete.

| **9** |

The Battle of the Whales

Two days later, we visited a strange place—an extinct volcano. Most of it was underwater. Only the top rose up into the open air. The sea had filled the wide cavity in the volcano's center. Now it looked much like a lake surrounded by mountains.

Captain Nemo explained that he got coal from the base of the volcano. From the coal, he got sodium, which he used to make electricity. Working underwater, Captain Nemo's men used shovels and axes to mine the coal.

"I'm anxious to continue our tour of the world's oceans," he told me. "My men dig coal for one day only. So if you wish to walk on the top of the volcano, it must be today."

Ned, Conseil, and I climbed over the rough volcanic stones. Only a few shrubs and fragrant flowers were growing there.

We had arrived at the foot of some sturdy trees when Ned Land exclaimed, "A hive!"

He quickly gathered dried leaves and lit a fire. Soon the bees were smoked out, and Ned put several honey cakes in his backpack.

Before we returned to the *Nautilus*, Ned also killed a sea bird with a stone. He was delighted to get some game for dinner.

The next day, we passed another body of water—the Sargasso Sea. This part of the Atlantic is as calm as a meadow. It's covered with a carpet of seaweed, along with floating trees and broken parts of ships. The currents are so slow here that nothing is washed away.

Around the middle of March, the *Nautilus* was heading south. Where were we going—to the South Pole? Surely that was madness.

Ned Land had become almost silent. He resented being imprisoned. When he met the captain, I could see the anger in his eyes.

I knew the monotony of being on board must be torture to Ned. But one day, as the *Nautilus* passed near a group of whales, his spirits suddenly brightened.

For a while we watched the whales from the platform. Ned's hand started to tremble as he lifted an imaginary harpoon. He asked the captain if he could hunt them.

"That would be killing for killing's sake," the captain replied. "I allowed you to kill the dugong—but only to get fresh meat for my crew. But we don't need whale oil on board the *Nautilus*. These southern whales already have plenty of natural enemies—the sperm whale, swordfish, and sawfish. And men, too, are helping to kill them off."

Ned Land turned away angrily. Captain Nemo pointed out to sea. "Do you see those black moving points about eight miles away? Those are sperm whales—terrible animals. Watch, I'll use the spur of the *Nautilus* to attack them."

I wondered at this. Attack a whale with a steel spur? Who'd ever heard of such a thing?

When the *Nautilus* went underwater, the battle between the southern whales and the sperm whales had already begun. We peered through the open panels as the submarine moved in on the whales with its terrible spear.

The massacre went on and on. An hour went by before the sea finally became calm again.

We rose up to the surface. The waters all around us were littered with the torn bodies of the sperm whales.

"Well, Master Land?" the captain asked.

"Well, sir," said Ned, "it is a terrible sight. I'm not a butcher—and I call this butchery!"

"It is a massacre of mischievous animals," Captain Nemo said. "And the *Nautilus*, sir, is not a butcher's knife."

Ned Land was furious with the captain. I decided to watch him closely.

Meanwhile, the *Nautilus* headed farther south. I wondered if Captain Nemo really did intend to reach the South Pole. I hoped not. Everyone who'd ever tried that journey had failed.

On March 14, we spotted icebergs. The captain carefully guided the *Nautilus* through the massive obstacles. Some sparkled like crystal. Other groups of icebergs looked like towns. When the ice fields blocked our way completely, the *Nautilus* would ram through like a wedge, making frightful cracking noises.

More than once, the submarine was in danger of getting stuck.

Captain Nemo *was* planning to go to the South Pole! And it was clear that he'd decided to travel there *under* the ice.

To prepare, the captain filled the reserve tanks with fresh air. Then the *Nautilus* went under the sea. We spent part of that first night at the window. The ocean floor was deserted here; there were no fish to see.

The next day, the *Nautilus* tried to rise to the surface again and again. Each time, it was blocked by tons of ice. Filled with hope and fear, I slept poorly that night. The *Nautilus* kept searching for an opening until about six o'clock in the morning. It was then I heard Captain Nemo cry out, *"The sea is open!"*

10

Attacked by Cuttlefish

I rushed to the platform. *Yes!* Now the sea was open, with only a few scattered icebergs.

As soon as we could take our bearings, we set off for the South Pole itself. It was a single island, rising about 100 yards above the water.

We reached the island by boat. Conseil was about to jump onto the land when I grabbed him. I said to Captain Nemo, "Sir, the honor of being the first to set foot on this land belongs to you."

"Yes, sir," the captain agreed. "And I won't hesitate to accept that honor. Up to this time, no human being has left a trace here."

After a few minutes ashore, he called us to join him. The soil was reddish, sandy stone. The air was filled with thousands of birds.

Captain Nemo put his hand on my shoulder. "I, Captain Nemo, on this 21st day of March, 1868, have reached the South Pole," he said proudly. "I hereby claim possession of this part of the globe." As the sun was setting, Captain Nemo marked the spot with his own black flag. A golden *N* for Nemo was its only decoration.

At three o'clock the next morning, I was thrown from my bed. The *Nautilus* had struck an enormous iceberg! The entire ship, as a matter of fact, was completely surrounded by a wall of ice.

Captain Nemo was as calm as ever. His plan was to find the thinnest ice and dig his way out. We had enough air to last for two more days.

We put on diving suits and began to dig. After 12 hours, we'd dug through only one yard of ice. At this rate, it would take more than four days to dig free! By this time, we had enough air for just one more day. And even as we worked, the ice was refreezing—and becoming thicker!

Captain Nemo had an idea. He heated the water in the *Nautilus*'s tanks until it was boiling hot. Then he pumped the hot water into the sea. For a while, the water around us grew warmer. Now, when we chipped away at the ice, it did not refreeze.

The next day, there was little air left in the reservoir. Breathing was so difficult that I felt weak and powerless. Brave Conseil murmured, "Oh, if only I could stop myself from breathing. Then master would have more air!"

When we were about six feet from the surface, our reservoir of air was nearly empty. Dizziness and pain made me feel like a drunken man. I was afraid that I was suffocating.

Finally, the ice cracked with a sharp noise.

"*We are free!*" Conseil declared.

As we broke the water's surface, the top door was opened wide. At last, pure air flooded into the *Nautilus*. We were saved!

Having accomplished its goal, the *Nautilus* left the South Pole with great speed. From there, we traveled to Cape Horn and on to the Amazon. Ned Land was disappointed that we never once came close to land.

On April 16, I realized how long we'd been prisoners on the *Nautilus*. I'd learned enough to write the true book of the sea. I did not wish to have this book buried with me. I wished it to be published!

On this same day, a number of huge cuttlefish—some 24 feet long—attacked us. These terrible creatures were armed with tentacles and great, sharp, parrot-like beaks. One of these monster fish even seized the propeller with its beak. The *Nautilus* could not move.

"Electric bullets are useless against them," Captain Nemo said. "Their flesh is too soft. But we shall attack them with hatchets."

He brought the *Nautilus* up to the surface. About ten men, including myself and Conseil, had armed ourselves with hatchets. Ned Land, of course, had seized a harpoon.

As the hatch opened, we could see 20 tentacles waving above us. When one long tentacle slid down the ladder, Captain Nemo cut it with his hatchet. We were rushing up the ladder when another tentacle seized a sailor and carried him away!

Hurrying after him, we saw that the poor man was hanging in the air with the tentacle wrapped around him. Captain Nemo flung

himself at the cuttlefish. He cut off one arm after another as the rest of the mutilated monster disappeared under the waves.

I thought Captain Nemo would be able to free the sailor once most of the arms had been cut off. But now the monster shot out a great stream of black ink. We were blinded for a moment. When we were able to see again, the cuttlefish had disappeared—along with the unfortunate sailor.

Covered with blood, Captain Nemo stared at the now empty sea and wept.

| 11 |

Escape from the Maelstrom

Captain Nemo grieved terribly over the death of the sailor. He let the *Nautilus* drift. It seemed that this might be a good time to escape—until the weather turned stormy. Then it was too dangerous to leave.

The *Nautilus* was heading toward Canada, Ned Land's home. Once more, Ned urged me to ask Captain Nemo for our freedom.

I knocked on the captain's door. "What do you want?" he barked.

"Please, sir," I said, "I must speak to you."

He turned to a manuscript on his table. "This manuscript," he said, "tells all I know of the sea—and it's also the history of my life. I'm going to shut it up in a watertight case. Then the last survivor of the *Nautilus* will throw it into to sea. It will end up wherever the waves happen to take it."

I was shocked. "But who knows where the waves will take it?" I asked. "Why not set us free, and I can deliver it—"

"*Never, sir!*" Captain Nemo thundered. "As I told you seven months ago, whoever enters the *Nautilus* must never leave it!"

Stunned, I left the room. I hurried off to find Ned and Conseil.

"The *Nautilus* will soon come close to New York," Ned said. "We will escape there—whatever the weather may be."

But on the 18th of May, we were hit by a cyclone. The terrible winds blew us far from land. Again, escape proved to be impossible.

Ned began to stay in his room. But one day I found him on the platform, along with Conseil and Captain Nemo. I had gone up there because I was puzzled by a noise I'd heard—a booming sound.

A ship was in the distance. It was a man-of-war, and it was firing at us! We couldn't tell which country it was from. But to Ned, it was clearly a possible means of escape.

To attract attention, Ned waved his handkerchief in the air. Seeing this, Captain

Nemo threw him down on the deck.

"*Fool!*" Captain Nemo roared. "Do you wish to die?"

Captain Nemo's face was deadly pale. He glared at the man-of-war and shouted, "Ah, ship of a cursed nation! I know which country you are from!"

I didn't know what to think. "Sir, are you going to attack that ship?" I asked.

"I am going to sink it," he snapped.

"Surely you won't do that!" I objected.

"I *shall* do it," he said in an icy voice. "Do not judge me, sir. You should not have seen this. Now, go below."

"Where is this ship from?" I asked.

"You do not know?" he bellowed. "Well, that's good! *Now, go below!*"

Captain Nemo didn't attack immediately. Instead, he let the ship chase him to the east. Hours later, I went up to the platform. The captain was talking to himself.

"I am the law! I am the victim—and I will have revenge! Because of these people I have lost everything. I've lost my country, my wife, my children, my father, and my mother. I saw all perish. All I hate is there. Say no more!"

I hurried back to Ned and Conseil. "We must escape now!" I cried out. "The man-of-war will be sunk very soon. If we don't get away, we'll be victims of Captain Nemo's revenge."

All night we waited. Finally, the second of June dawned, a dreadful day.

The *Nautilus* slowed its speed. It was allowing the man-of-war to come close. For us, it was time to escape. We hurried to the boat. But just then, the *Nautilus* was going underwater. We were too late!

Then the *Nautilus* began to rush forward. I felt a shock—and screamed. Its deadly spur had pierced the unfortunate vessel as easily as a needle pierces cloth!

Through the panels, I saw the man-of-war sinking. Desperate people ran around the deck. The mast of the sinking ship passed before my eyes. Then it sank out of sight.

When it was over, I saw Captain Nemo enter his room. I watched as he stood before a portrait of a woman with two little children. Then he stretched out his arms toward them, knelt down, and burst into sobs.

I felt a chill of disgust for Captain Nemo. Whatever these people had done to him, he had no right to punish them so viciously.

Some hours later, Ned came to my bunk and woke me. "We will escape tonight," he whispered. "There is land—20 miles to the east. I don't know which country it is."

"Yes, Ned," I said, "we shall try—even if the sea should swallow us up."

I dressed in warm clothes and collected my notes. From the captain's room, I heard the sounds of the pipe organ. I was terribly afraid of meeting Captain Nemo. A single word from him might chain me on board.

Creeping past his door, I heard him sigh, then sob again. Then I heard him murmur, "Enough! *Enough!* "

I rushed to the stairs and found Ned and Conseil waiting there.

"Let's go!" I whispered.

We climbed into the boat. Ned began to unfasten the bolts that held it to the *Nautilus*. Then we heard men shouting. I felt Ned slip a dagger into my hand.

But the men were not looking for us.

In one voice they were shouting, "The *maelstrom*!"

The maelstrom! That deadly whirlpool! That meant we must be near the dangerous coast of Norway. Had Captain Nemo brought us here on purpose?

Caught in the whirlpool, the *Nautilus* began to spin wildly. We clung to the boat.

"We must hold on to the *Nautilus*!" Ned said. "Don't let the bolts be loosened!"

But the bolts gave way with a dreadful wrenching noise. Torn from its groove, the boat was hurled like a stone into the midst of the whirlpool.

My head struck a piece of iron, and I lost all consciousness.

* * * *

So ends our voyage under the seas. How we happened to escape from the whirlpool that night, I cannot tell.

When I came to, we were in a fisherman's hut, in Norway. Ned Land and Conseil were holding my hands. We are waiting here for a ship to take us home.

I have continued to write of our adventure.

Who has more right than I to speak of these seas? In not quite 10 months, I have crossed 20,000 leagues in a submarine tour of the world. Shall I be believed? I don't know—and it matters little, after all.

What has become of the *Nautilus*? And Captain Nemo? If he still lives, I pray that the wonders of the seas will somehow soothe his vengeful spirit. Peace is my hope for us all.

BOOK SEQUENCE

First complete the sentences with words from the box. Then number the events to show which happened first, second, and so on.

Conseil	country	bone	stare
bracelet	Aronnax	coconut	cabin
crewmen	breadfruit	Ned Land	library
deck	savages	submarine	welcomes
platform	sinks	damages	Captain Nemo

____ 1. Captain Nemo orders Aronnax to return to his _____.

____ 2. Aronnax is thrown overboard when two huge spouts of water flood the

_____.

____ 3. Nemo and his second lieutenant _____ into the distance.

____ 4. The "thing" strikes and _____ the Scotia.

____ 5. Eight men take the visitors inside the

_____.

____ 6. Commander Farragut _____ Aronnax to the Abraham Lincoln.

____ 7. Ned Land slices and roasts some

_____.

____ 8. In the coral kingdom, _____ form a semicircle around Captain Nemo.

____ 9. Captain Nemo shows Arronax his

_____.

____ 10. _____ realizes that their food had been drugged.

____ 11. _____ resists wearing a diving suit.

____ 12. _____ points out a recent shipwreck.

____ 13. Conseil shatters a _____ on a savage's arm.

CHARACTER STUDY

Reread Chapter 2 and answer below.

A. Circle two words that describe each character.

1. **Captain Nemo**

   musician   humble   mournful   timid

   merciful   average   secretive   clever

2. **Pierre Aronnax**

   Canadian   doctor   professor   regretful

   elderly   curious   artist   writer

3. **Ned Land**

   impatient   hesitant   trickster   scientist

   strong   skillful   passive   determined

3. **Conseil**

   fickle   calm   selfless   aggressive   obedient

   hilarious   uncomplaining   unpredictable

CAUSE AND EFFECT
Reread Chapter 3 and answer below.

A. Write a letter to match each *cause* on the left with its *effect* on the right.

CAUSE

1. ___ While waiting, Ned Land becomes terribly hungry.

2. ___ The *Nautilus* is attacked by the *Abraham Lincoln*.

3. ___ Captain Nemo says his visitors must remain in their cabins at certain times.

4. ___ Captain Nemo reads some books written by Pierre Aronnax.

5. ___ Huge reservoirs on the *Nautilus* store air.

EFFECT

a. The crew can stay underwater for long periods of time.

b. Aronnax resents being treated as a prisoner.

c. He grabs the first servant he sees by the throat.

d. The captain claims the right to treat his attackers as enemies.

e. He offers to teach Aronnax even more about the sea.

B. Answer the questions in your own words.

1. What was the **effect** of the *Nautilus's* steel hulls?

_____

_____

_____

_____

_____

2. What was the **effect** of Nemo's offer to show Aronnax the underwater "land of marvels"?

_____

_____

_____

_____

_____

_____

RECALLING DETAILS

Reread Chapter 6 and circle a letter to answer the question or complete the sentence below.

1. The weapons carried by the savages were
   a. stones and arrows.
   b. long, pointed spears.

2. How did Aronnax, Conseil, and Ned Land escape the savages?
   a. By hiding
   b. In a boat

3. What was Captain Nemo doing when Aronnax found him on the Nautilus?
   a. Visiting his museum
   b. Playing the pipe organ

4. What rare specimen did Aronnax and Conseil find in the sea?
   a. A coral formation
   b. An unusual shell

5. What did Captain Nemo think would happen at high tide?
   a. The Nautilus would be set free.
   b. The weather would suddenly improve.

COMPREHENSION CHECK

Reread Chapter 10 and write T or F to show whether each statement is
true or *false*.

1. _____ Conseil was the first to set foot on the
South Pole

2. _____ To mark the spot, Captain Nemo planted
a black flag.

3. _____ The crewmen dug through only one
yard of ice.

4. _____ Conseil and Ned Land feared they were
suffocating.

5. _____ From the South Pole, the Nautilus headed
for Cape Cod.

6. _____ The largest cuttlefish may be 15 feet long.

FINAL EXAM

A. Circle a letter to complete the sentence or
answer the question.

  1. Who did Captain Nemo proclaim was "free from
  men at last"?
  a. Pierre Aronnax
  b. The dead crewman

  2. Who disagreed with Aronnax about Captain
  Nemo's true motives?
  a. Ned Land
  b. Conseil

3. Who rescued the Indian pearl diver from a shark attack?
   a. Ned Land and Pierre Arronax
   b. Captain Nemo and Ned Land

4. The huge dugong is related to which more familiar sea mammal/
   a. manatee
   b. orca

5. Where did Captain Nemo get his gold ingots?
   a. from wrecks of Spanish ships
   b. from pirate treasure chests

6. What resource did Captain Nemo harvest from the extinct volcano?
   a. coal
   b. magma

B. Answer each question in your own words. Write in complete sentences.

1. Captain Nemo approved of killing animals for what two reasons?

   _____

   _____

   _____

   _____

   _____

   _____

   _____

   _____

2. The events in this fictional journey took place in the late 1860s. At that time, little was known about the deep seas. Since then, what scientific advances have made the oceans' depths much less mysterious?

_____

_____

_____

_____

_____

_____

_____

_____

Answers to Activities
20,000 Leagues Under the Sea

BOOK SEQUENCE
1. 10/cabin   2. 3/deck   3. 11/stare   4. 1/damages
5. 4/submarine   6. 2/welcomes   7. 8/breadfruit
9. 13/crewmen   10. 5/library   11. 12/Aronnax
12. 6/Ned Land   13. 7/Conseil   14. 9/Bracelet

CHARACTER STUDY
1. musician, mournful, secretive, clever
2. doctor, professor, curious, writer
3. impatient, skillful, strong, determined
4. selfless, obedient, calm, uncomplaining

CAUSE AND EFFECT
A.   1. c   2. d   3. b   4. e   5. a
B.   1. They could resist water pressure and prevent puncture.
2. It made Aronnax forget about regaining his freedom for the time being.

RECALLING DETAILS
1. a 2. b 3. b 4. b 5. a

COMPREHENSION CHECK
1. F   2. T   3. T   4. F   5. F   6. F

FINAL EXAM
A.   1. b   2. b   3. b   4. a   5. a   6. a
B.   1. for food or to protect endangered species from extinction by vicious predators
2. Inventions such as radar and sonar have given us much more factual information about the deep seas.